Dear Parent:

Congratulations! Your child is taking the first steps on an exciting journey. The destination? Independent reading!

STEP INTO READING® will help your child get there. The program offers five steps to reading success. Each step includes fun stories and colorful art. There are also Step into Reading Sticker Books, Step into Reading Math Readers, Step into Reading Phonics Readers, Step into Reading Write-In Readers, and Step into Reading Phonics Boxed Sets—a complete literacy program with something to interest every child.

Learning to Read, Step by Step!

Ready to Read   Preschool–Kindergarten
• big type and easy words • rhyme and rhythm • picture clues
For children who know the alphabet and are eager to begin reading.

Reading with Help   Preschool–Grade 1
• basic vocabulary • short sentences • simple stories
For children who recognize familiar words and sound out new words with help.

Reading on Your Own   Grades 1–3
• engaging characters • easy-to-follow plots • popular topics
For children who are ready to read on their own.

Reading Paragraphs   Grades 2–3
• challenging vocabulary • short paragraphs • exciting stories
For newly independent readers who read simple sentences with confidence.

Ready for Chapters   Grades 2–4
• chapters • longer paragraphs • full-color art
For children who want to take the plunge into chapter books but still like colorful pictures.

STEP INTO READING® is designed to give every child a successful reading experience. The grade levels are only guides. Children can progress through the steps at their own speed, developing confidence in their reading, no matter what their grade.

Remember, a lifetime love of reading starts with a single step!

Copyright © 2012 Disney Enterprises, Inc. All rights reserved. Published in the United States by Random House Children's Books, a division of Random House, Inc., 1745 Broadway, New York, NY 10019, and in Canada by Random House of Canada Limited, Toronto, in conjunction with Disney Enterprises, Inc.

Step into Reading, Random House, and the Random House colophon are registered trademarks of Random House, Inc.

Visit us on the Web!
StepIntoReading.com
randomhouse.com/kids

Educators and librarians, for a variety of teaching tools, visit us at RHTeachersLibrarians.com

ISBN: 978-0-7364-2885-9 (trade) — ISBN: 978-0-7364-8112-0 (lib. bdg.)

Printed in the United States of America 10 9 8 7 6 5 4 3 2 1

STEP INTO READING®

STEP 3

Disney
FAIRIES

SECRET
of the
WINGS

New Friends

By Kitty Richards

Illustrated by the Disney Storybook Artists

Random House 🏠 New York

One day in Pixie Hollow,
Tinker Bell and her friends
were making snowflake baskets.

When they were done,
snowy owls took the baskets
to the Winter Woods.
Winter fairies needed them
to collect snowflakes.
Tink watched the owls fly.
She wished she could visit
the Winter Woods, too.

Warm fairies could not go
to the Winter Woods.
The cold hurt their wings.
Winter fairies could not go
to the warm side of Pixie Hollow.
The heat could
wilt their wings.

Tinker Bell was curious.

She went with Fawn

to the border of the Winter Woods.

It was time for the animals

to cross into winter.

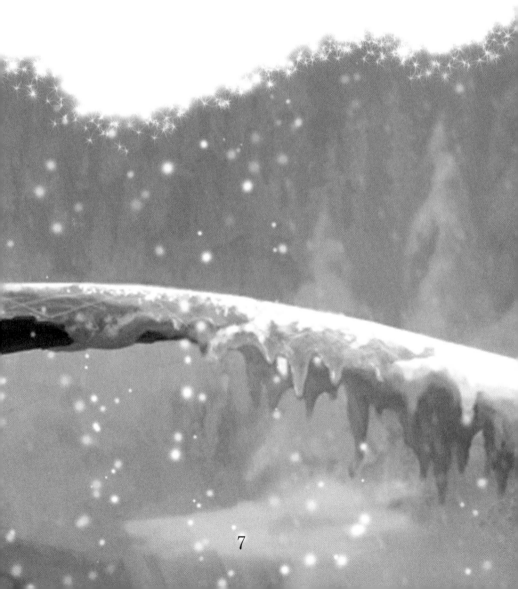

While Fawn was busy,

Tink snuck across the border.

Winter was very cold

and very pretty.

Suddenly,

Tink's wings began

to sparkle!

They glowed

with a bright light.

Tink could not stay in winter.

Her wings would freeze.

She went back home.

Tink wanted to know

why her wings had sparkled.

She went to the library.

There was a book about wings.

The author's name was the Keeper.

He lived in the Winter Woods.

Tink bundled up.

She hid

in a snowflake basket.

She was going

to find the Keeper!

Tink's basket landed
in the Winter Woods.
She hid from the winter fairies.
But her book fell out!

The ruler of winter saw it.

His name was Lord Milori.

"Return this book to the Keeper,"

he told a fairy.

Tink could follow the fairy

to the Keeper!

Tink followed the fairy

to the Hall of Winter.

The Keeper was there.

A frost fairy also rushed in.

Her name was Periwinkle.

Tink and Peri
flew near each other.
Their wings began
to sparkle and shine.
The Keeper smiled.
"Follow me!" he said.

The Keeper took Tink and Peri
to a magical room.
It showed images from their past.
Both fairies had been born
from the same laugh!

The laugh had split in two.
Tinker Bell had gone
to the Pixie Dust Tree.
Periwinkle had gone
to the Winter Woods.
They were sisters!

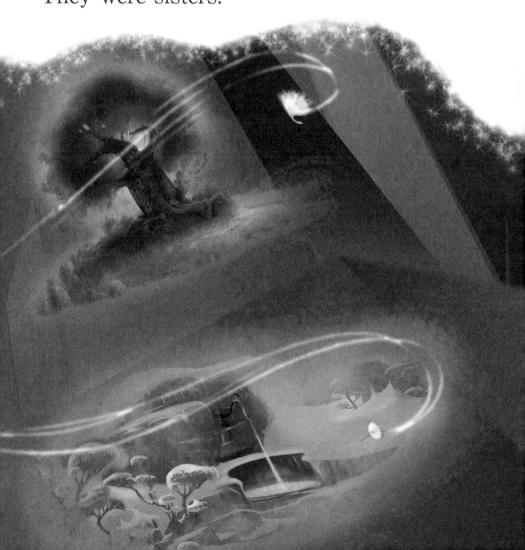

Just then,
Lord Milori entered.
"If he sees you,
he'll send you back!"
Peri told Tink.
The sisters hid.

The Keeper spoke
to Lord Milori.
When the lord left,
the Keeper told Tink
to go home before moonlight.

Tinker Bell and Periwinkle
spent the day together.
Peri showed Tink her collection
of Lost Things.
"I call them Found Things,"
the frost fairy said.

Peri and her friends
took Tinker Bell sledding.
Tink was so happy!
She didn't want the day to end.

It grew late.

Tink built a fire.

She told Periwinkle

about the warm seasons.

"I wish I could go there,"

Periwinkle said.

Crack!

The fire melted the ice

under Tink and Peri!

The sisters fell.

The Keeper and his pet lynx

saved them just in time.

The Keeper told Tink
it was time
to go home.
The sisters hugged good-bye.

They had a plan
to see each other again.
"Meet me here tomorrow,"
Tink whispered.

Back at home,
Tinker Bell told her friends
about her sister.
They built a snow machine
so Peri could visit them.

They took the machine
to the border.
Periwinkle brought ice.
The machine would use the ice
to make snow.
The snow would keep
Peri cold in the warm seasons!

Periwinkle crossed the border.
When she flew under the machine,
snowflakes circled her wings.

The snow machine worked!

Peri's wings would be safe

on the warm side of Pixie Hollow.

Tinker Bell showed Periwinkle
all her favorite places.
They floated down a stream.

Peri flew in a meadow.

They visited Tink's friends.

Rosetta gave Periwinkle a flower.

Peri waved her hand over it.

She covered the flower with frost.

The icy coating would protect it

so she could take it home.

Soon the day got warmer.

The snow machine

ran out of ice.

Periwinkle felt weak.

Her wings started to droop.

"I think they're too warm,"
she said.
Peri had to get back
to the Winter Woods!

Queen Clarion and Lord Milori
were waiting
at the border.
They were very worried.
Periwinkle crossed over.

Her wings got better.

"This is why we

do not cross the border,"

Lord Milori told the sisters.

"You two may never

see each other again."

Tink and Peri were heartbroken.

Lord Milori flew off
on his owl.
He pushed the snow machine
into the water.

Tink went with Queen Clarion

to her chambers.

The queen told Tink that

the border rule had been made

to keep fairies safe.

Tink was very sad.

Suddenly,

she saw a snowflake outside!

It was snowing in Pixie Hollow!
Tink and her friends flew
to the border.
The snow machine was stuck
on a waterfall.

It wouldn't stop making snow!
The fairies pushed and pulled.
They got the machine loose,
but it was too late.
Pixie Hollow was going
to freeze!

If the Pixie Dust Tree froze,

it couldn't make pixie dust.

No fairy would ever fly again!

Suddenly,

Tink remembered Peri's flower.

Under the frost,

it had been safe.

Tink had an idea.

She flew to the Winter Woods

and found the winter fairies.

Tinker Bell asked the winter fairies
to frost the Pixie Dust Tree.
They followed Tink
and got to work.

The freeze had already begun.

"Their frost can protect the tree,"

Tink told Queen Clarion.

The fairies waited
for the freeze to pass.
Finally, the sun came out.
The warmth melted the frost
from the tree.
It began to make
pixie dust again!

The Pixie Dust Tree was safe.

But Tink's wing was broken!

It had frozen when she flew

to the Winter Woods for help.

Tinker Bell and Periwinkle were sad.

They held their wings together.

Suddenly, the sisters' wings
sparkled more than ever.
When the glow faded,
Tink's wing was healed!

Everyone was happy!

Now the warm fairies could

have their wings frosted

and visit the Winter Woods anytime.

Best of all,

Tinker Bell and Periwinkle

would never be apart again.